P9-DOB-498

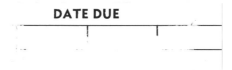

DATE DUE

Peggy Parish

MIND YOUR MANNERS!

illustrated by
Marylin Hafner

A Mulberry Paperback Book
New York

10 9 8 7 6 5 4 3 2

Library of Congress Cataloging-in-Publication Data
Parish, Peggy. Mind your manners! / Peggy Parish ; illustrated by Marylin Hafner.
p. cm.
Summary: An introduction to proper manners for meeting new people, receiving
gifts, using the telephone, dining out, and other common social situations.
ISBN 0-688-13109-3
1. Etiquette for children and teenagers. [1. Etiquette.]
I. Hafner, Marylin, ill.   II. Title.   BJ1857.C5P37 1994
395'.122—dc20   93-11732   CIP   AC

FOR PAIGE AND BILL DuBOSE,
WITH LOVE—P. P.

FOR MY MOTHER,
WITH LOVE—M. H.

Contents

Contents

Manners!

Grown-ups always say,

But why?

What can be the use of them?

They are such a bother.

But good manners
can mean good fun.
They make you
a nice person to know.
Here are some manners
you should learn.

Meeting New People

Your parents are proud of you.
They like their friends
to meet you.
When you are introduced,
shake hands.
Say something friendly,
such as
"It's nice to meet you."

Manners with Grown-ups

When grown-ups
come into a room,
stand up until they are seated.
Hold doors open for them.
Let them go through first.

Always use Mr., Mrs., or Ms.
with their names.
This is one way to show
your respect for them.

Telephone Manners

When you answer the telephone,
say, "This is . . ."
and give your name.
If the caller wants
to speak with someone else,
say, "Just a moment, please."

Then find the person.
If that person is out,
say so and ask,
"May I take a message?"
Always write down messages.

When you call a friend,

say, "This is . . ."

and give your name.

"May I speak to . . ."

and give your friend's name.

If you dial a wrong number,
say, "I'm sorry."
Then hang up gently.

Visiting Manners

Visiting is fun.

People like to have you

when you mind your manners.

Never touch anything

without asking if you may.

If you and a friend
take out toys,
help with clean-up
before you leave.
Always thank your friend
for having you visit.
Thank your friend's parent, too.

When friends visit you,
let them choose what to play.

Your parents

also have friends visit.

Greet them nicely.

If you do not want to stay,

quietly ask your parents

if you may leave.

Eating Out

Eating out is special.

Decide what you want to order.

And stick with it.

Talk quietly while you wait

for the food.

If you finish first,

wait for the others.

A restaurant is not

a place to play.

When you leave,

thank whoever invited you

for a nice time.

That means your parents as well!

Sleep-overs

Staying overnight
with a friend is fun.
Be sure to take
everything you need.
After a meal try to say
something nice about it.

23

Let your friend's parents
know you enjoyed the food.
For instance, say,
"That was good."

Offer to help with clean-up.
Do as your friend's parents
ask you to do.

Table Manners

Learn table manners at home.

Before you go to the table,

wash your hands and face.

Brush your hair.

When you sit down,

put your napkin on your lap.

Learn to use a knife and fork.

Always say, "Please,"

when you ask for something.

Chew your food

with your mouth closed.

Don't try to talk

while you are chewing.

When you finish eating,
put your knife and fork
on your plate.
If your napkin is a paper one,
put it on the table.
If it is a cloth napkin, fold it.
Then put it on the table
or in your napkin ring.

Always ask,

"May I be excused?"

before you leave the table.

Party Manners

When you have a party,
really use your best manners.
Greet your guests as they come in.
Be sure everyone knows
everyone else.

Plan your party well.

Have lots of things to do.

Help each guest find something
that is fun.

A busy party is a happy party.

If it's your birthday,

you blow out the candles

on the cake.

You cut the cake.

But your guests are served first.

When you go to a friend's party,
be a good sport.
Play the games that are planned.
Try to be nice to everyone.
When you leave, thank your friend
for inviting you.

Please & Thank You

"Please" and "thank you"
are very good words.
Learn to use them.
When you ask for something,
start by saying, "Please."
If you get what you want,
always say, "Thank you."

When someone
offers you something, say,
"Yes, please," if you want it.
If you don't want it,
say, "No, thank you."

Receiving Gifts

When someone gives you a gift,
always say, "Thank you."

When someone sends you a gift,
write a thank-you note.
You may not like the gift.
But you must thank the person
for thinking of you.

Grown-up Parties

Parents have parties, too.

Many times you can help.

You can make things for the party.

You can help in serving the food.

Hold the plate carefully.

Ask the guests if

they would like some.

If anyone has
an empty glass or plate,
ask if you may get that guest
more to drink or eat.

Taking Turns

In games be fair.

Wait for your turn.

Don't rush other people.

Let them take their time.

Your turn will come.

Interrupting

When someone else is talking,
don't interrupt.
Wait until he or she has finished.
Then say what you want
to tell or ask.
When everyone talks at once,
no one is heard.

Secrets, Tattling, & Gossip

Everybody loves a secret.
It's fun to share one
with a good friend.
But wait until you can be alone
with your friend.
It may hurt others' feelings
if you whisper to one person.

Do not be a tattletale.

Let people talk for themselves.

You do not like anyone

to tattle on you.

Sometimes you and a friend
have a quarrel.
You may want to say
awful things about your friend.
Don't do it.
That's called gossip.

People may tell other people
what you said.

They may add things to it.

And you may lose your friend forever.

Never say anything about a person

that you wouldn't say to the person.

Shopping Manners

Stores have so much to see in them.

But just look.

Don't touch unless you plan to buy.

Stay with the grown-up

who brought you.

Stores are not places
to run around in.
They are not places
to shout in.
Show your respect
for other shoppers.

Use Your Eyes

Watch where you are going.

At home, on the street, in stores,

there are other people.

If you do not watch,

you may run into them.

Someone may get hurt.

If you do bump into anyone,

always say, "I'm sorry."

Coughing & Sneezing

Cover your mouth
when you cough or sneeze.
When you sneeze,
you scatter germs.
If you have a cold,
someone else may get it.

Chewing Gum

Chew gum with your mouth closed.
Many people do not like
to see gum-chewing.
Never blow bubble gum in public.
Do it alone. Or do it
with other bubble-gum blowers.

You begin learning manners
as a baby.
Your parents help you.

They teach you
to wash your hands
before you eat.
They brush your hair.
They teach you to say
"please" and "thank you."

Manners grow with you.

When you use them,

they become a part of you.

This book tells you the manners

you should be using now.

As you grow older,

you will learn others.

Good manners are very important.

They make you

a nice person to know.